STAR WARS
THE
MANDALORIAN
HANDBOOK

STAR WARS
THE
MANDALORIAN
HANDBOOK

Written by Matt Jones

CONTENTS

INTRODUCTION

While the Empire may have been defeated, the new galactic government, named the New Republic, does not have complete control over the galaxy, particularly in the Outer Rim. Groups of Imperial forces are operating in the area, and members of the Bounty Hunters Guild track down criminals for money.

Following the Great Purge of Mandalore, the Mandalorian people are few in number and scattered across the galaxy, hiding in their coverts. One Mandalorian bounty hunter plies his risky trade in the Outer Rim.

THE MANDALORIAN

The best in the parsec

The Mandalorian, or Mando for short, is a bounty hunter in the Outer Rim and part of the Nevarro covert. Mando is a member of the Bounty Hunters Guild and is well respected for his success at his job. He uses his pay to support the covert.

Things you need to know about the Mandalorian

1 Mando's real name is Din Djarin. As a child, he was rescued from a battlefield by a unit of Mandalorians.

2 He then became a foundling and was raised to become a Mandalorian warrior.

3 Mando believes strongly in a set of rules known as the Way. Not all Mandalorians believe the same thing.

4 His armor has some pieces made of pure beskar. He gains new pieces of armor as he travels around the galaxy.

Sensors at back of ship

WEAPONS CABINET

Mando keeps a range of blasters in a cabinet on his ship. He allows his allies to use these weapons if they need to.

Engine

Cockpit

Mk 3e/W heavy
laser cannon

THE *RAZOR CREST*

The Mandalorian flies a battered old gunship
named the *Razor Crest* around the galaxy. It is
equipped with a range of gear that helps him
work as a bounty hunter. The ship even has
a carbon-freezing chamber that he uses to put his
targets in stasis so they are easier to transport.

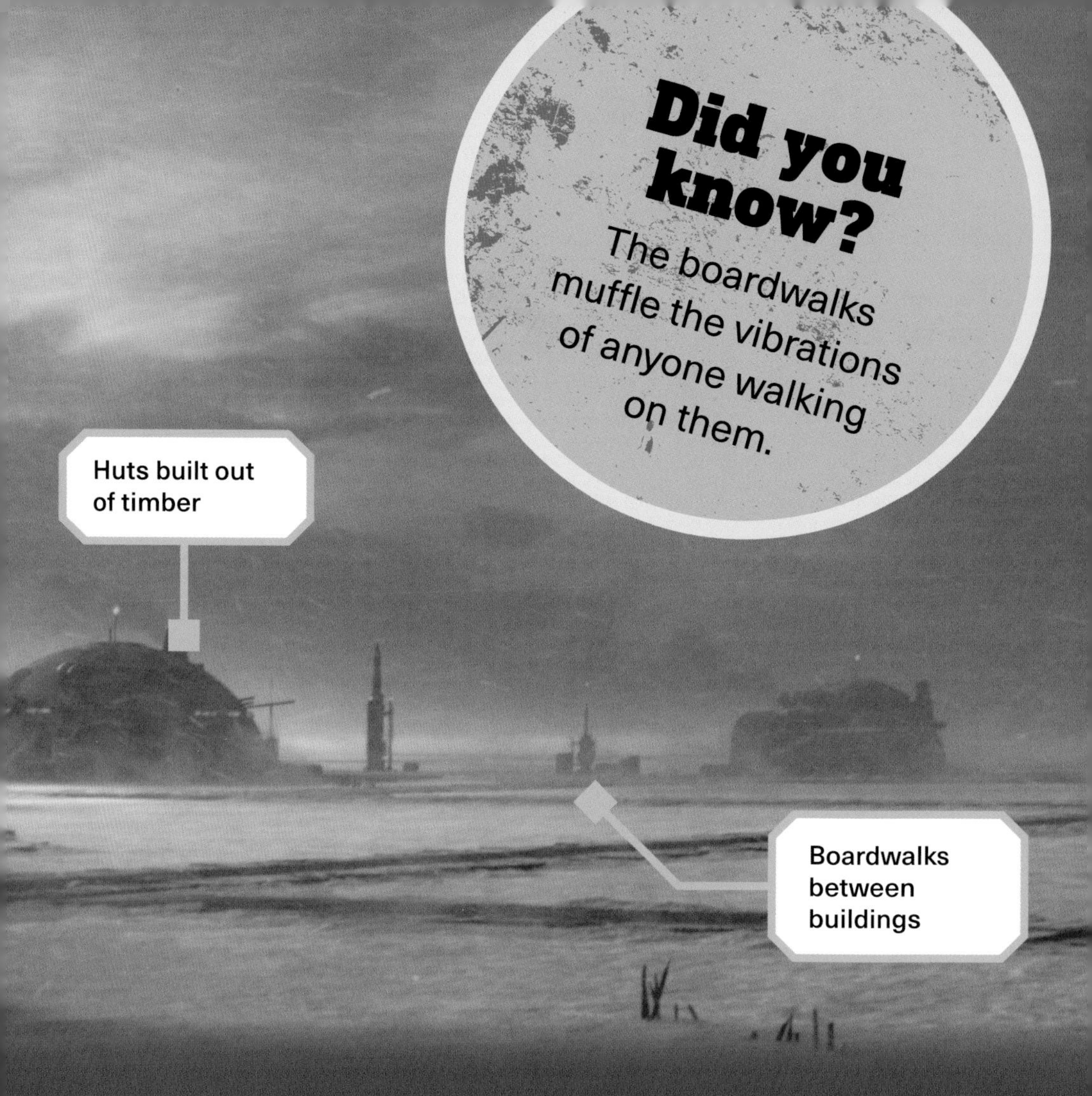

Huts built out of timber
Boardwalks between buildings

Did you know?
The boardwalks muffle the vibrations of anyone walking on them.

PAGODON

An icy world in the Outer Rim, Pagodon is a perfect place to hide. Mando visits the planet to track down a criminal. A number of locals are involved in the trawling trade, trying to catch the shoals of fish under the ice.

Hut holds communication equipment

Empty building

FERRYMAN'S REACH

There is a small settlement on Pagodon called Ferryman's Reach. The outpost has sixteen buildings, including a public house for the trawlers to relax in.

THE MYTHROL

Mando's target

This friendly Mythrol is a criminal. He lied and stole money on Nevarro so he fled the planet. The criminal is hiding on Pagodon among the local trawlers when he first meets Mando. The bounty hunter uses a piece of equipment called a tracking fob to locate him.

Things you need to know about the Mythrol

1 Mando's tracking fob is a short-range sensor. It contains data on this Mythrol's chain code and beeps when he is nearby.

2 The Mythrol carries a range of credits in the purse on his belt and tries to bribe Mando to let him go.

3 The Mythrol is a skilled computer slicer.

4 The Mythrol is given the chance to work off his crimes by Greef Karga on Nevarro.

RAVINAKS

Watch out for these vicious predators! These beasts lurk beneath the ice sheets on Pagodon and erupt to devour any prey they can get their tusks into.

Muscly body moves quickly through water

Sharp claws

Powerful tail

Tusks are valued by some hunters

RAVINAK ATTACK

When a ravinak latches onto one of the *Razor Crest*'s landing struts, Mando has to act quickly. He shoots the beast with his disruptor rifle and dislodges the pest.

Buildings blend into surroundings

City gate used to have a bell

Basic landing area outside the city

NEVARRO

Nevarro is a planet in the Outer Rim and has many volcanoes. There used to be an Imperial base on the planet, but many believe that the Empire left the world when it was defeated by the Rebel Alliance. The local Bounty Hunters Guild boss is Greef Karga, who is based in Nevarro City.

Did you know?

A group of Mandalorians hides underground in a place known as a Mandalorian covert.

Red awnings adorn the local bazaar

NEVARRO CITY

Nevarro City has a number of places of interest, including a local bazaar, a public house, an Imperial Remnant safe house, and a secret Mandalorian covert.

GREEF KARGA

Guild Boss

Greef Karga is a charming and successful boss of the Bounty Hunters Guild. Based out of a cantina in Nevarro City, Greef hands out bounties to his fellow Guild members. His favorite hunter is Mando because he is one of the best!

Things you need to know about Greef

1 Greef Karga used to be Nevarro's Magistrate until he had to leave his role.

2 He is a good shot with a blaster pistol.

3 Greef does not like the Empire and doesn't want any Imperials on Nevarro.

4 He becomes Magistrate again after Mando defeats Moff Gideon.

5 Greef is determined to improve Nevarro and wants its people to have a prosperous future.

THE CLIENT
This Imperial leader operates from a small safe house in Nevarro City. He is known only as the Client by the bounty hunters he has hired to capture the asset.

THE IMPERIAL REMNANT

The Empire was defeated years ago. However, groups of Imperial troops are still found on worlds across the Outer Rim. These forces are known as the Imperial Remnant, but it is not clear if they are all independent groups or a united force.

Did you know?

While the safe house may be small, there's a sizable Imperial base outside the city.

DOCTOR PERSHING

Doctor Pershing is a nervous scientist who is working at the safe house on Nevarro. He's involved in some secret projects and needs the asset for his experiments.

THE ARMORER

This is the Way

The Armorer is a wise member of the Mandalorian covert on Nevarro. She helps maintain her fellow Mandalorians' weapons and armor and also crafts new items for them.

Things you need to know about the Armorer

1 The Armorer on Nevarro is known only by her title.

2 Mandalorians respect armorers and listen to their advice.

3 Beskar is a rare metal found naturally on some worlds in Mandalorian space.

4 Only Mandalorian armorers can craft beskar into suits of armor.

5 While the Armorer normally uses her tools for smithing, she can also use them to defend herself from Imperials.

Jawa sandcrawler

ARVALA-7

There's not much of note on this muddy planet, but Mando travels here on the hunt for the asset. Some individuals have settled on Arvala-7. At least one brave clan of Jawas has moved to the planet, and a Nikto gang has taken over an abandoned compound where it guards the asset.

Track leads toward mudhorn cave

BLURRGS

These animals are found on many worlds, including Ryloth, the Forest Moon of Endor, and Arvala-7. Blurrgs are not the smartest beasts, but they make good steeds.

KUIL

Ugnaught ally

Kuiil is an Ugnaught mechanic who lives on Arvala-7. He maintains his own farm and seeks a peaceful life without any disturbances. When a criminal gang sets up nearby, Kuiil is willing to help Mando if he gets rid of them.

Things you need to know about Kuiil

1 He is an incredible mechanic and repairs Mando's heavily damaged ship.

2 Kuiil is also very good at mending droids. He fixes up damaged bounty hunter droid IG-11 and trains the droid to help him.

3 He has a number of blurrgs that he keeps as farm animals.

4 Kuiil likes Grogu and gives his life trying to protect him from the Empire.

IG-11

By the Code

IG-11 is a member of the Bounty Hunters Guild and is also tasked with tracking the asset on Arvala-7. IG-11 beats Mando to the asset's location, but they work together until IG-11 tries to kill the asset. Mando then shoots the droid!

Things you need to know about IG-11

1 IG-11 is an IG-series assassin droid. Another model in the line is IG-88, who is a more infamous bounty hunter.

2 His programming means that he must self-destruct if there is a chance he will be defeated in combat.

3 An Ugnaught named Kuiil repairs IG-11 and trains him to become a ranch hand and protector.

4 IG-11 makes the ultimate sacrifice, giving his life to protect Grogu from the Imperial Remnant.

GROGU

The Child

The asset is a curious youngling who is strong with the Force and has a big appetite. Mando meets this child named Grogu on Arvala-7. Grogu becomes very attached to Mando and will do whatever he can to protect him.

Things you need to know about Grogu

1 Grogu belongs to a species that is rarely seen in the galaxy. Most known members appear to be strong with the Force.

2 He can use the Force to perform incredible feats, from lifting heavy animals to stealing tasty treats from fellow kids.

3 Grogu is actually 50 years old, but he is still young for his species!

4 Grogu is very eager to try and eat anything he can get his hands on!

Canopy can quickly cover its occupant

GROGU'S PRAM

Grogu has a special hover pram to help him keep up with Mando's faster pace. His pram has a built-in repulsor so it can hover above the ground, and Mando can control it remotely.

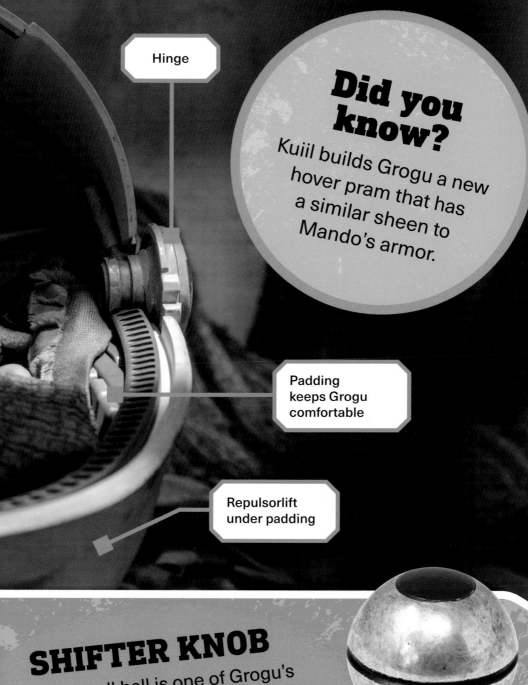

Hinge

Padding keeps Grogu comfortable

Repulsorlift under padding

SHIFTER KNOB

This small ball is one of Grogu's favorite things on the *Razor Crest*. It should be attached to an important control in the cockpit, but Mando lets Grogu play with it.

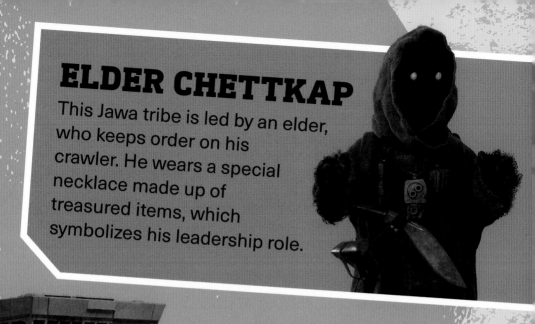

ELDER CHETTKAP

This Jawa tribe is led by an elder, who keeps order on his crawler. He wears a special necklace made up of treasured items, which symbolizes his leadership role.

Jawa-sized cockpit

Loading ramp

SANDCRAWLER

Sandcrawlers were built on Corellia by the Corellia Mining Corporation and used in many places. On Tatooine, the vehicles were originally used in mining operations. They were then abandoned, so tribes of Jawas made the crawlers their homes. Some Jawas have taken their vessels offworld and settled on other planets, such as Arvala-7.

MUDHORN

Found on Arvala-7, mudhorns are very strong and dangerous creatures. They use caves as their nests. If an intruder enters their homes, they use their horns as weapons to defend themselves.

Fur is always covered with mud

MUDHORN EGGS

A female mudhorn produces eggs. A clan of Jawas on Arvala-7 loves the taste of the eggs, which they call sooga. Mando brings them one in exchange for parts stolen from him.

Strong teeth for hardy diet

Trees surround the village

Hut belongs to a villager named Caben

COMMON HOUSE

Dara Vish is the owner of a common house on Sorgan. She has created a warm and friendly atmosphere. Some of her regulars travel far to visit.

Barn

Did you know?

Sorgan does not have any starports, so Mando lands in a forest clearing.

Equipment for brewing spotchka

SORGAN

Sorgan is a densely forested world that is estimated to have fewer than 10,000 inhabitants. The world has no cities, so it is an ideal place for Mando to lay low after the events on Nevarro.

OMERA

Omera is a krill farmer. When raiders attack her village, she is willing to fight back. Omera is one of the few in her village who know how to shoot a blaster.

Did you know?

The drink made from krill is named spotchka and is popular offworld.

KRILL FARMERS

On the forest world of Sorgan, many locals make a living by farming small crustaceans called krill. These blue animals can be used to make a range of things from a dye to a beverage. One village has farmed krill for generations.

WINTA
Omera's daughter Winta is fun and kind. She has many friends in the village and enjoys playing with Grogu.

CARA DUNE

Alderaanian fighter

Cara Dune is a strong warrior who is one of Mando's allies. She used to be part of the Rebel Alliance. Cara really doesn't like Imperials because they destroyed her homeworld, Alderaan, during the Galactic Civil War.

Things you need to know about Cara Dune

1 Cara is very strong and a great warrior. She often uses a blaster rifle in combat and is also skilled in unarmed fighting.

2 Cara Dune used to be a dropper—a specially trained trooper who went on dangerous missions.

3 Cara still wears pieces of her armor from her Rebel Alliance uniform.

4 She tells Mando that she left the New Republic forces because she was bored with the lack of action after the Empire's defeat.

45

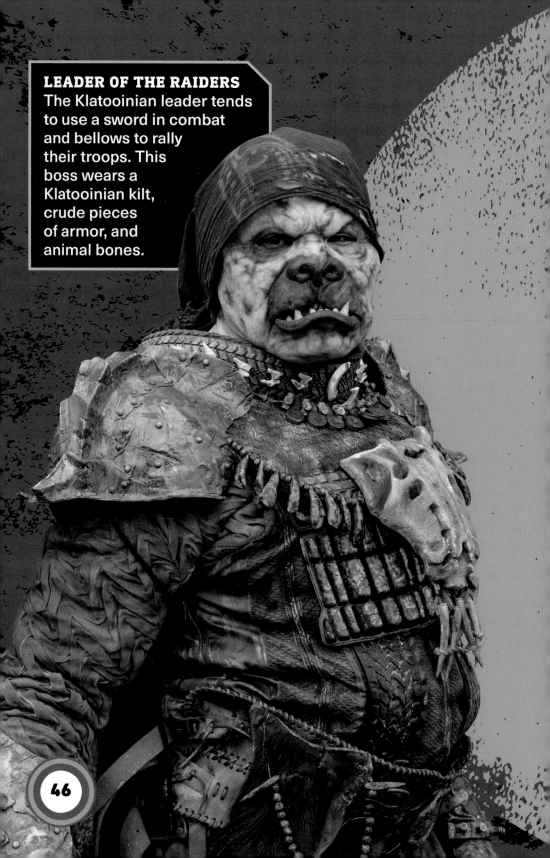

LEADER OF THE RAIDERS

The Klatooinian leader tends to use a sword in combat and bellows to rally their troops. This boss wears a Klatooinian kilt, crude pieces of armor, and animal bones.

KLATOOINIAN RAIDERS

This fearsome gang keeps raiding the poor krill farmers on the Outer Rim planet Sorgan. These aggressive Klatooinians really enjoy a local beverage named spotchka, so they steal the farmers' produce to brew their own.

RAIDER BASE

The Klatooinians have a base on Sorgan. They can be found relaxing here, drinking spotchka between raids. None of them expect to be attacked themselves by Mando and Cara Dune.

Did you know?

The raiders are rumored to have attacked other worlds.

Viewport

Twin laser cannon

Did you know?

AT-STs are manufactured by a company called Kuat Drive Yards.

SCARY SIGHT

At night this AT-ST looks very evil, with red light shining out of its viewports. Thankfully, the vehicle is destroyed by Cara Dune in battle.

Knee joint has nonstandard plating

Painted by the raiders

RAIDER AT-ST

The raiders have an old Imperial vehicle at their disposal. It is an All Terrain Scout Transport (or AT-ST), which walks on two legs and is equipped with powerful blasters. While it hasn't been repaired to Imperial standards, the AT-ST is still a formidable vehicle that strikes fear into experienced warriors Cara Dune and Mando.

RIOT MAR

Riot Mar is a member of the Bounty Hunters Guild. He is hunting down the Mandalorian. Mar is an experienced pilot and flies a customized ship.

Engine

Cockpit

Communications antenna

FINAL FLIGHT

Above Tatooine, Riot Mar engages Mando in the *Razor Crest*. While Mar scores a hit, Mando destroys Mar's starfighter.

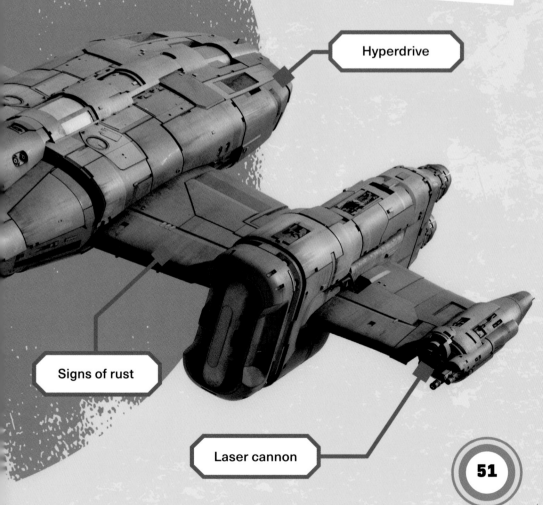

Hyperdrive

Signs of rust

Laser cannon

PELI MOTTO

Mos Eisley mechanic

Peli Motto owns Docking Bay 3-5 in Mos Eisley on Tatooine. She collects rent from any docked starships and offers a range of other services. A number of droids work for Peli, including a trio of pit droids and astromech droid R5-D4.

Things you need to know about Peli Motto

1 Peli can repair and refuel a ship, but the cost will be higher if the owner doesn't want droids to be involved.

2 She knows a lot of local gossip, so can offer tips on the latest news in Mos Eisley.

3 Peli enjoys the card game sabacc and practices with her pit droids in the bay.

4 She keeps a range of equipment on her tool belt and has a scanner to assess the state of ships.

5 Peli also has a WED treadwell droid.

TORO CALICAN

Aspiring hunter

Toro Calican is a brash young man who wants to be a famous bounty hunter. He has a tracking fob for dangerous mercenary Fennec Shand and teams up with Mando to capture her.

Things you need to know about Toro Calican

1 Toro Calican is not experienced at bounty hunting, and Mando has to save his life multiple times on the mission.

2 Toro owns a pair of brand new quadnoculars. He can use this piece of technology to look at things in the distance.

3 For the trek into the desert, Toro drives a 712-AvA speeder bike that was built by the Aratech Repulsor Company.

FENNEC SHAND

Legendary mercenary

Fennec Shand is a highly skilled mercenary who has worked in the galactic underworld for decades. When Fennec meets Mando on Tatooine, they are enemies. However, they later become allies on Tython and work together.

Things you need to know about Fennec Shand

1 Fennec is nimble and moves quickly around the battlefield.

2 Her favorite weapon is a sniper rifle, which she can use at any range.

3 Following the events on Tatooine, Fennec has mechanical organs that keep her alive.

4 Fennec often wears a helmet that she has owned for decades.

5 Shand has worked for the Hutts.

RANZAR MALK

Former colleague

Ranzar Malk and Mando used to work together as mercenaries. Nowadays, Malk does not go on missions and runs an illegal starship repair business out of a space station named the Roost.

Things you need to know about Ranzar Malk

1 The Roost space station does have some shielding, but it lacks weaponry so is vulnerable to attack.

2 Malk owns a *Rogue*-class starfighter that has been upgraded to modern starfighter standards.

3 His team has worked on many ships over the years, including the *Razor Crest*.

4 Ran Malk also oversees a group of mercenaries.

MIGS MAYFELD

Sharpshooting mercenary

Migs Mayfeld used to be an Imperial sharpshooter, but he left the Empire toward the end of the Galactic Civil War. He now works for Ranzar Malk and leads Malk's mercenary crew on missions.

Things you need to know about Mayfeld

1 Mayfeld is unbelievably accurate with a blaster. He was an elite trooper in the Imperial Army.

2 Migs wears a special backpack on his shoulder that has a metal arm. He can use his mind to operate the arm and fire a third blaster.

3 Mayfeld is sent to the Karthon Chop Fields by the New Republic, where he has to serve a sentence of 50 years.

4 Migs left the Imperial army because he hated seeing his fellow soldiers dying during missions toward the end of the war.

Male Devaronians have horns

BURG
Burg is a brawny Devaronian. He is very strong and enjoys rushing into combat and throwing enemies around.

Blades have very sharp edges

XI'AN
Xi'an is a Twi'lek warrior who specializes in melee weapons. She carries daggers that she can throw at her targets.

MALK'S CREW

Malk has put together a small team for a prison-break mission. Each crew member has unique skills or attributes that will be useful. The unruly crew is led by Migs Mayfeld and joined by the Mandalorian.

A droid's eyes are called photoreceptors

Q9-0
Q9-0, or Zero, is a former protocol droid who has now turned to a life of crime. He is the crew's pilot and stays aboard the *Razor Crest*.

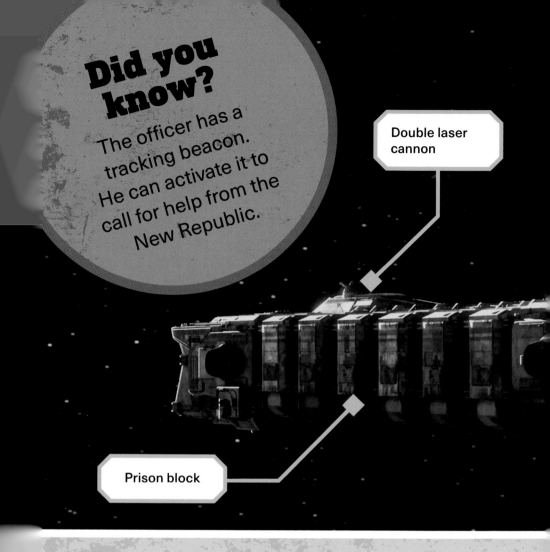

Did you know?

The officer has a tracking beacon. He can activate it to call for help from the New Republic.

Double laser cannon

Prison block

BOTHAN-5

The *Bothan-5* is a New Republic prison ship, responsible for transporting and holding prisoners. The ship is crewed by New Republic Correctional Corps officer Lant Davan and a number of security droids. Malk's crew wants to liberate prisoner X-6-9-11, who turns out to be another old colleague of Mando's.

Sensor dish

CEC-5900hh ion engine

QIN

Xi'an's brother Qin is the prisoner the team wishes to free. Qin hates Mando for leaving him behind on a previous mission, which led to his imprisonment.

Did you know?

Reptavians have poisonous claws that can be lethal!

Armored scales on top of neck and back

Sharp canines for eating meat

Powerful legs can carry heavy loads

HUNTED HUNTERS

A flock of reptavians attack Mando and the group he is traveling with. They make off with a blurrg and a Trandoshan hunter.

Wingspan is
11.44 m
(37 ft 6 in)

REPTAVIAN

Reptavians are batlike creatures that are native to Nevarro. They have sharp claws and teeth and are very quiet when hunting at night. Reptavians hunt in flocks for food that they take back to their young.

MOFF GIDEON

Powerful commander

Moff Gideon is a smart and mysterious Imperial leader. He commands a number of Imperial Remnant forces and really wants to capture Grogu for an unknown reason.

Things you need to know about Moff Gideon

1 Moff Gideon used to be a member of the Imperial Security Bureau, a part of the Empire that captured traitors and Rebel Alliance spies.

2 During the Imperial era, a Moff was a leader who oversaw a sector of the galaxy for Emperor Palpatine.

3 He participated in the Great Purge of Mandalore and ordered many deaths.

4 Gideon wields the Darksaber, a special lightsaber that is very important to Mandalorians and their history.

OUTLAND TIE FIGHTER

While normal TIE fighters can land on their wings, it is not ideal and is a nonstandard maneuver. TIE fighter pilots usually land at Imperial locations, which have equipment to assist them. The outland TIE fighter has collapsible wings and landing struts, so is far more versatile and can be used on planets where such luxuries are not readily available.

TIE wing in landing position

GIDEON

Moff Gideon likes to keep his skills sharp, so will often transport himself in his outland TIE fighter on missions. He joins the attack on Mando and his allies.

Open hatch

SFS L-s7.2 laser cannon

Landing strut

Armor has a cryaplast coat to protect its wearer

Scuffed paintwork

D-72w Oppressor flame projector

Flametroopers have red markings

Did you know?

There were flametroopers in the Grand Army of the Galactic Republic.

HOUSE ON FIRE

The interior of the Nevarro Common House goes up in flames quickly. Without the help of Grogu's Force powers, Mando and his allies would not survive.

FLAMETROOPER

The Empire had a number of specialist soldiers, including flametroopers, for different types of battlefields or specific missions. Flametroopers can be used to flush enemies out of a defensible position. They are trained to use flamethrowers and wear heatproof armor.

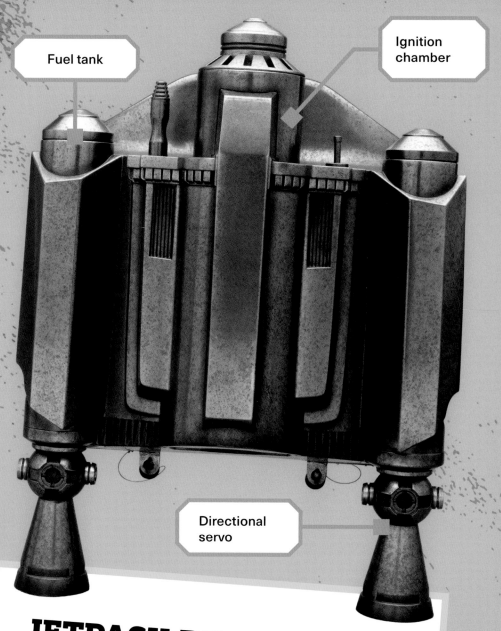

Fuel tank

Ignition chamber

Directional servo

JETPACK DESIGN

The Armorer is skilled in a range of crafts, including the maintenance and creation of jetpacks. She has used the armor from fallen Mandalorians to make this jetpack.

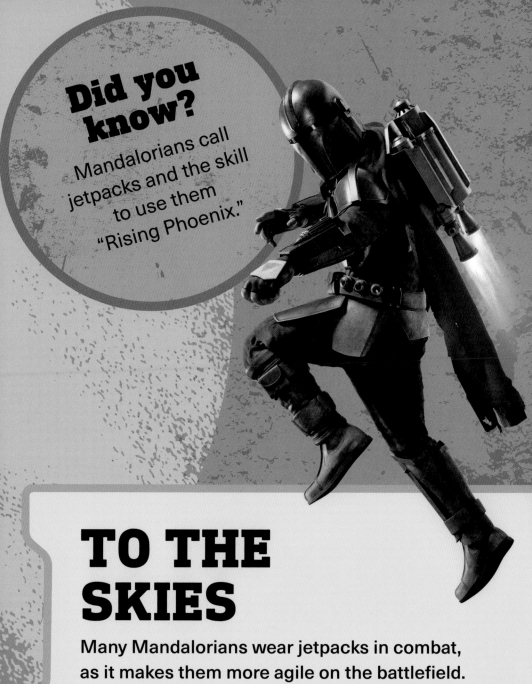

Did you know?

Mandalorians call jetpacks and the skill to use them "Rising Phoenix."

TO THE SKIES

Many Mandalorians wear jetpacks in combat, as it makes them more agile on the battlefield. The Mandalorian is given a beskar-plated jetpack by the Armorer when he returns to the covert on Nevarro. He soon takes to the skies to defeat Moff Gideon in his outland TIE fighter.

Saloon

Cobb's custom speeder

MOS PELGO

Mos Pelgo is a small mining settlement on Tatooine that has suffered since the Empire's fall. Its residents were ruled over by the Mining Collective until they were rescued by local Cobb Vanth in a suit of Mandalorian armor.

Equipment measures wind speed

Drinking trough

LOCAL SALOON

Mando encounters Cobb Vanth in the local saloon. The bartender has a range of beverages available, including spotchka.

COBB VANTH

The Marshal

Cobb Vanth was born on Tatooine and wants to help the people that live there. He purchased a suit of Mandalorian armor from some Jawas, which he wears to defend the town of Mos Pelgo. Vanth meets Mando in the town's saloon.

Things you need to know about Cobb Vanth

1 Vanth owns a custom speeder that is a single Radon-Ulzer 620C podracer engine with a seat and some controls bolted on.

2 Cobb is the Marshal of Mos Pelgo and is responsible for protecting its residents.

3 Like many individuals on Tatooine, Vanth does not trust Tusken Raiders.

4 He wields a KA74 blaster rifle and an HF-94 heavy blaster pistol.

5 His suit of armor used to be worn by infamous bounty hunter Boba Fett.

TUSKEN RAIDERS

Survival experts

Tusken Raiders are from Tatooine and live in the world's harsh deserts. The others that live on Tatooine see Tuskens as vicious and violent, but they have not taken the time to learn much about them.

Things you need to know about Tuskens

1 Tusken Raiders are also known as Sand People by moisture farmers.

2 Tusken Raiders are nomadic, which means they don't have a permanent home and move around.

3 Massiffs are doglike creatures that have been tamed by Tusken Raiders and guard their camps.

4 The gaderffii, or gaffi stick, is a Tusken weapon that they often wield in combat.

5 Tuskens fear krayt dragons.

Horns

84

BANTHAS

The bantha is an animal found on Tatooine. They produce tasty blue milk that many moisture farmers like to drink. Tusken Raiders often ride banthas in single file across Tatooine's deserts, and treasure the beasts.

Did you know?

Tusken Raiders consider banthas to be members of their tribes.

Thick fur

KRAYT DRAGON

Krayt dragons are terrifying monsters that stay under the sand and emerge to devour their prey. There are a number of krayt dragon species on Tatooine, and the largest ones can grow to at least 184 m (604 ft) long!

Tail helps the dragon move under the sand

This krayt dragon has sixteen limbs

Bony armor on head

Mouth can emit harmful ichor

TO KILL A KRAYT

The residents of Mos Pelgo and a tribe of Tusken Raiders work together to take down a krayt dragon on Tatooine. While the plan goes awry, they still manage to kill the dangerous creature.

87

FROG LADY

Very important passenger

Known only as Frog Lady on Tatooine, this individual is desperate to reunite with her partner on the moon named Trask. Mando transports her on the *Razor Crest*, but the trip doesn't go according to plan!

Things you need to know about Frog lady

1 Frog Lady keeps her last eggs in a special, temperature-controlled backpack. They are very delicate and will be destroyed if Mando's ship enters hyperspace.

2 Frog Lady is an excellent shot with her Shard-3A holdout cluster blaster and is also a proficient droidsmith.

3 She has a long tongue that she can use to grab things far away from her.

4 Frog Lady can also hop if she needs to move quickly, especially when she's being chased by hungry ice spiders!

CARSON TEVA

X-wing pilot

Carson Teva is a member of the New Republic Navy who helps ensure order in parts of the Outer Rim. He worries that the Imperial Remnant still operating in the area might become a big problem for the New Republic.

Things you need to know about Carson Teva

1 Carson often flies alongside fellow pilot Trapper Wolf.

2 Teva flies a T-65 X-wing on his patrols around the Outer Rim.

3 He carries an A280 blaster rifle in his X-wing and is a good shot.

4 Carson helps Mando, Grogu, and Frog Lady when they are attacked by ice spiders on Maldo Kreis.

5 He is based at a New Republic outpost on Adelphi.

Passage leads to a hot spring

Electrical sparks

HOT SPRINGS

Maldo Kreis is very cold. However, there is at least one hot spring on the planet, which forms a haven for a colony of hibernating ice spiders.

MALDO KREIS

Maldo Kreis is a planet that does not appear
to have been explored extensively. Ice covers
the planet, which has canyons and caves
carved out of the surface. Making a stop
on Maldo Kreis is not part of Mando's plan!

ICE SPIDERS

Vicious arachnids

Known only as ice spiders, these terrifying creatures lurk in caves on Maldo Kreis. Many different life stages of the spiders hibernate together near a hot spring on the planet and chase down any prey in unison.

Ice spiders appear to develop additional legs as they mature

HATCHLINGS

Upon hatching, ice spiders appear to show an instinctive and ravenous hunger. Some even attempt to eat Grogu!

Stomach

Multiple rings
of teeth

Did you know?

Similar arachnid creatures lurk on the planets Dagobah, Atollon, and Taul.

Walkers help with port operations

TRASK

Far from the New Republic's reach, Trask is an oceanic world inhabited by Mon Calamari and Quarren colonists who want to get away from the politics on their homeworld. Mando visits the world to reunite Frog Lady with her partner and to meet other Mandalorians.

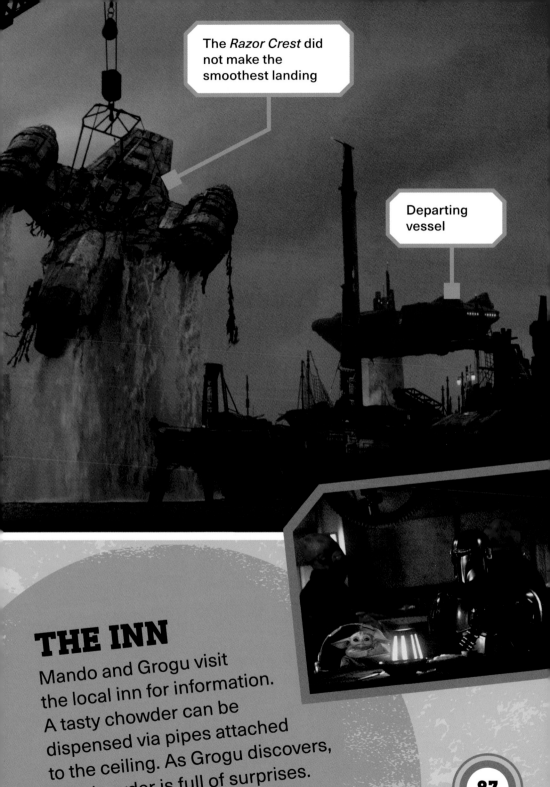

The *Razor Crest* did not make the smoothest landing

Departing vessel

THE INN

Mando and Grogu visit the local inn for information. A tasty chowder can be dispensed via pipes attached to the ceiling. As Grogu discovers, the chowder is full of surprises.

QUARREN SHIP

The captain of this Quarren fishing vessel offers to take Mando to meet other Mandalorians. The scheming captain is lying, but he inadvertently attracts the attention of Mandalorian Bo-Katan Kryze and her unit.

Mast

Mamacore
The sailors keep a captive mamacore in their hold. It tries to eat Grogu!

Ship's bow

QUARREN CREW

The ship's Quarren crew is in on the captain's attempt to kill Mando. Mando's beskar armor is a more valuable catch than their standard haul of fish.

Mamacore cage

Upper deck

Engine

BO-KATAN KRYZE

Nite Owl leader

Bo-Katan Kryze is a Mandalorian leader and warrior. She has fought for her people for decades. Bo-Katan wants to reclaim her homeworld of Mandalore.

Things you need to know about Bo-Katan

1 She is a powerful fighter who wields WESTAR-35 blasters in combat.

2 Her sister Duchess Satine Kryze used to rule Mandalore until her death.

3 Bo-Katan disagreed with her sister's views that Mandalorians should be peaceful and not warriors.

4 Bo-Katan was the leader of a group of warriors named the Nite Owls.

5 She wants to reclaim the Darksaber as it can be used to unite the Mandalorians.

KRYZE'S UNIT

Bo-Katan Kryze used to command an army, but those times have passed. For the mission to steal an Imperial freighter on Trask, Bo-Katan leads a small Mandalorian team. The other members are Axe Woves, Koska Reeves, and a new recruit—Mando.

AXE WOVES
Axe Woves is a skilled Mandalorian warrior. He uses a data spike to break into the Imperial freighter.

TEAM TACTICS

Members of Bo-Katan's unit are highly trained and work together seamlessly. The stormtroopers on the freighter are no match for this team.

Did you know?

Mando is shocked when these Mandalorians take off their helmets in front of others.

KOSKA REEVES

Koska Reeves excels at hand-to-hand combat. She can perform powerful flying kicks with the help of her jetpack.

103

Laser cannon

Engine

FREIGHTER CAPTAIN

The captain of the freighter is very loyal to Moff Gideon. He tries to destroy the ship to stop the Mandalorians from taking it.

IMPERIAL FREIGHTER

The Empire used to have a number of *Gozanti*-class freighters to transport goods between worlds or even TIE fighters into battle. Moff Gideon's forces still use at least one of these freighters in the Outer Rim. It makes a tempting target for Bo-Katan's Mandalorian unit.

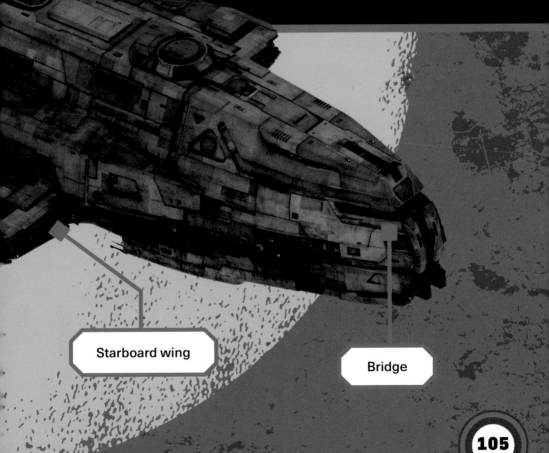

Starboard wing

Bridge

Model of
a planet

NEVARRO SCHOOL

Once a bounty hunting bar, the building at the crossroads in Nevarro City is now a school for the local kids. Grogu joins the class for a lesson on the geography of the galaxy, including key trade routes, capital planets, and the Kessel system.

Diagram of the Kessel system

NEVARRO TREATS

Grogu is far less interested in the lesson than he is in a fellow pupil's snacks. Grogu cannot focus until he uses the Force to get the tasty treats into his claws.

Turbolaser

SECRET PROJECT

Greef's group soon discovers that the base contains a laboratory. Dr. Pershing has been carrying out mysterious experiments on various test subjects.

Landing zone

Did you know?

The base is powered by volcanic activity deep underground.

IMPERIAL BASE

Greef Karga and Cara Dune ask for Mando's help to destroy a nearby Imperial base on Nevarro. Karga thinks the base will be nearly empty, but they discover that numerous stormtroopers, scout troopers, pilots, and scientists are still stationed here.

TREXLER MARAUDER 906

The Trexler Marauder 906 is a hovering tank used by the Empire. While the vehicle is based on the Imperial troop transport or ITT, it has far more firepower than the ITT as it was built to engage other vehicles in battle. A Trexler Marauder 906 is quite a rare sight—not that many were made.

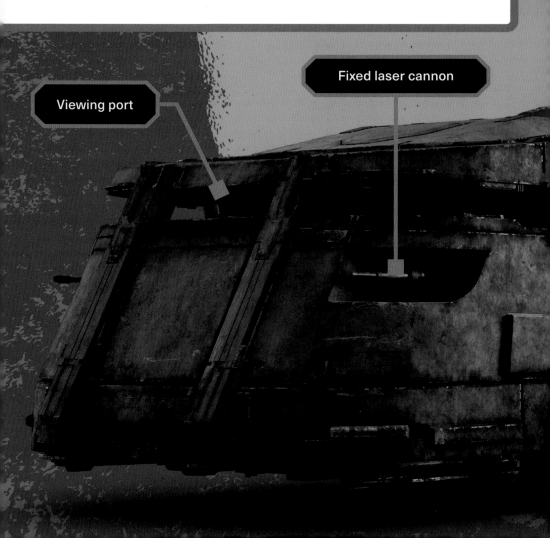

Viewing port

Fixed laser cannon

GUNNER POSITION

There is a gunner's station at the back of the vehicle. Its sensors are similar to ones found on some starships, which help the gunner target enemies.

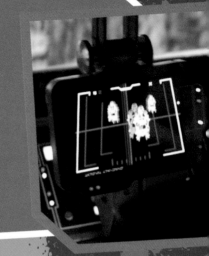

Strong armor

Laser turret

Signal beacon

Scout guard on the city's walls

CORVUS

This world in the Outer Rim has suffered under the cruel reign of the evil Morgan Elsbeth. Corvus used to be a heavily forested world, but Elsbeth has started to strip the planet of its trees.

Elsbeth's home

CALODAN

The city of Calodan is where Morgan Elsbeth resides. This walled city is guarded by her forces, and its people live in fear of her.

AHSOKA TANO

Former Jedi

Ahsoka Tano is a wise and powerful Force-sensitive who fights for good in the galaxy. She has played a vital role in galactic history and has known Bo-Katan Kryze for many years.

Things you need to know about Ahsoka

1 Ahsoka used to be a member of the Jedi Order and was Anakin Skywalker's Padawan.

2 The Jedi leaders kicked Ahsoka out of the Order when she was accused of being a criminal. Anakin proved her innocence, but she didn't want to rejoin the Jedi.

3 During the Imperial era, she worked with rebel leaders to unite various rebel groups into what would become the Rebel Alliance.

4 Ahsoka is on Corvus to find out the location of Thrawn from Morgan Elsbeth.

MORGAN ELSBETH

Calodan's Magistrate

Magistrate Morgan Elsbeth is a cruel leader who used to strip planets of resources for the Imperial fleet. After the Empire's fall, she continues these horrible acts, but it isn't clear where the pillaged resources are heading.

Things you need to know about Morgan Elsbeth

1 Morgan owns a spear of pure beskar which she offers to Mando if he can capture Ahsoka Tano.

2 She is well-versed in combat techniques and holds her own for a time against a highly trained lightsaber duelist.

3 Morgan is very calculating. She orders her troops to kill Calodan's civilians, but Mando manages to save them.

4 After Morgan is defeated by Ahsoka, Wing becomes Calodan's Magistrate.

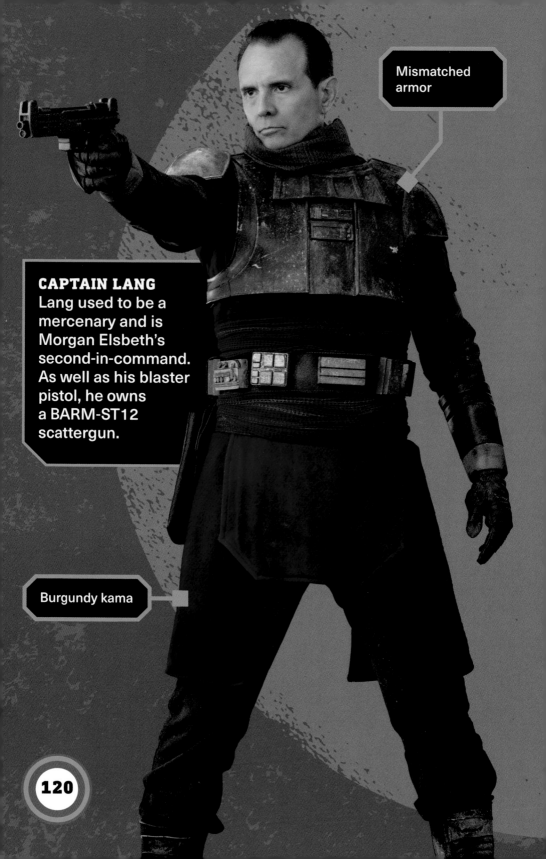

Mismatched armor

CAPTAIN LANG
Lang used to be a mercenary and is Morgan Elsbeth's second-in-command. As well as his blaster pistol, he owns a BARM-ST12 scattergun.

Burgundy kama

Did you know?

Elsbeth is also protected by a pair of HK-87 assassin droids.

Breathmask

SCOUT GUARDS
Elsbeth's scout guards patrol Calodan and the surrounding forests. They are no match for former Jedi Ahsoka Tano.

ELSBETH'S FORCES

Magistrate Morgan Elsbeth has a number of troops at her command. She uses these forces to instill fear into Calodan's residents and fight off anyone who might try to oppose her.

Old megalith

TYTHON

This ancient planet is very strong in the Force. There is an old temple atop a rocky outcrop, and Mando and Grogu visit the place in an attempt to call to a Jedi to help Grogu.

SEEING STONE

At the center of the temple there is a mysterious rock carved with ancient text. When Grogu sits atop it, he is surrounded by a barrier and cannot be reached by Mando.

BOBA FETT

Legendary bounty hunter

Boba Fett is a legendary name in the criminal underworld and has been a bounty hunter for decades. The motivations of the man under the helmet may sometimes be mysterious, but he helps Mando rescue Grogu as part of a deal.

Things you need to know about Boba Fett

1 His father, Jango Fett, provided his DNA for the clone troopers of the Republic.

2 Jango requested one unaltered clone, Boba. The younger Fett does not like being compared to the clone troopers.

3 Boba was trained from childhood to be a bounty hunter and is one of the greatest.

4 Jango was a Mandalorian foundling, so Boba is viewed by some as a Mandalorian.

5 Boba possesses Tusken Raider weapons.

BOBA FETT'S SHIP

Boba Fett inherited this *Firespray*-class ship from his father, Jango Fett, and the vessel has been in operation for decades. The ship has been modified by both Fetts and has many hidden weapons to surprise Boba's prey.

Repulsor wings pivot when landing

FETT AT THE HELM

Jango Fett taught Boba how to pilot the vessel when he was young. Boba is an amazing pilot and able to complete daring maneuvers in space or in the atmosphere.

Green-and-red paint job matches Boba's armor

Canopy

Rotating blaster

Yellow markings denote specialization

Merr-Sonn Munitions 201 mortar

COMPACT BACKPACK

Shell troopers have backpacks that they use to carry the ammunition for their mortars. The weapons fire thermal detonators.

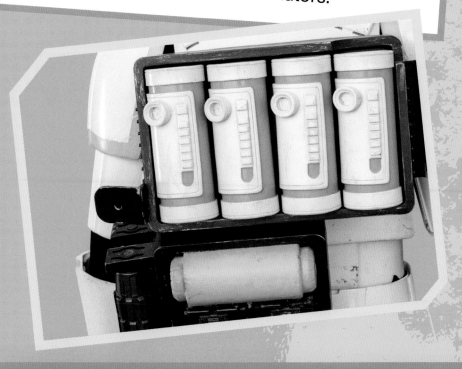

MORTAR TROOPERS

Mortar troopers, or shell troopers, are a special type of stormtrooper trained to use mortars on the battlefield. A mortar trooper is part of a squad that attacks Mando on Tython.

DARK TROOPERS

These scary battle droids are named dark troopers. They are very powerful and hard to defeat in combat. Moff Gideon's dark troopers are third generation units and were manufactured by the Imperial Department of Military Research.

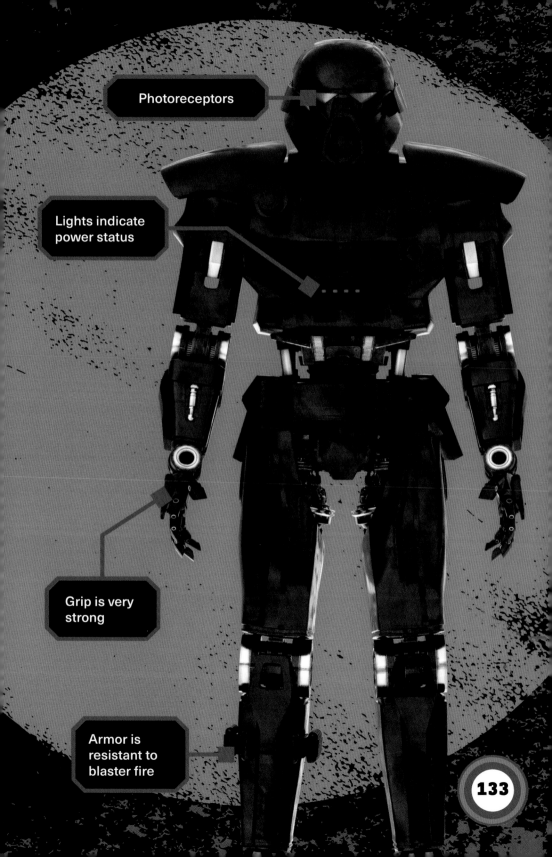

Photoreceptors

Lights indicate power status

Grip is very strong

Armor is resistant to blaster fire

133

Mayfeld in prison worker attire

Scrap metal

KARTHON CHOP FIELDS

The Karthon Chop Fields are a New Republic site where prisoners are used as laborers and are overseen by N5 sentry droids. Migs Mayfeld ends up here after Mando leaves him in a New Republic prison cell, and is later rescued by Mando as well.

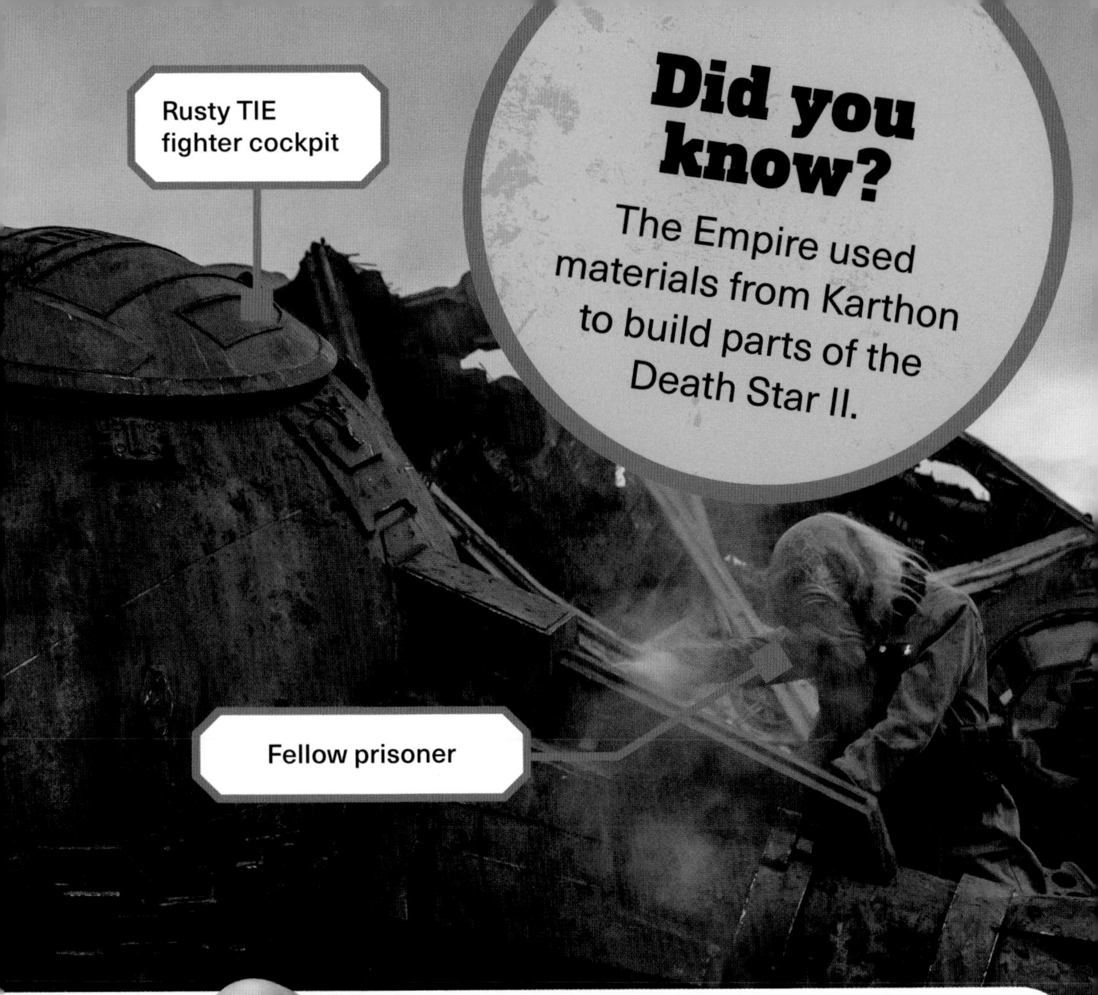

Rusty TIE fighter cockpit
Fellow prisoner

Did you know?

The Empire used materials from Karthon to build parts of the Death Star II.

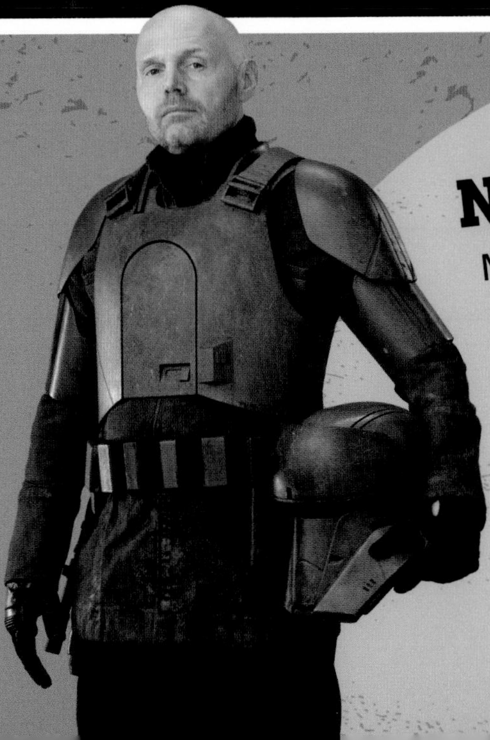

NEW MISSION

Migs' knowledge of Imperial protocols makes him a key asset in Mando's quest to retrieve Grogu from Moff Gideon. Migs proposes that they infiltrate a refinery on Morak to find out Grogu's location.

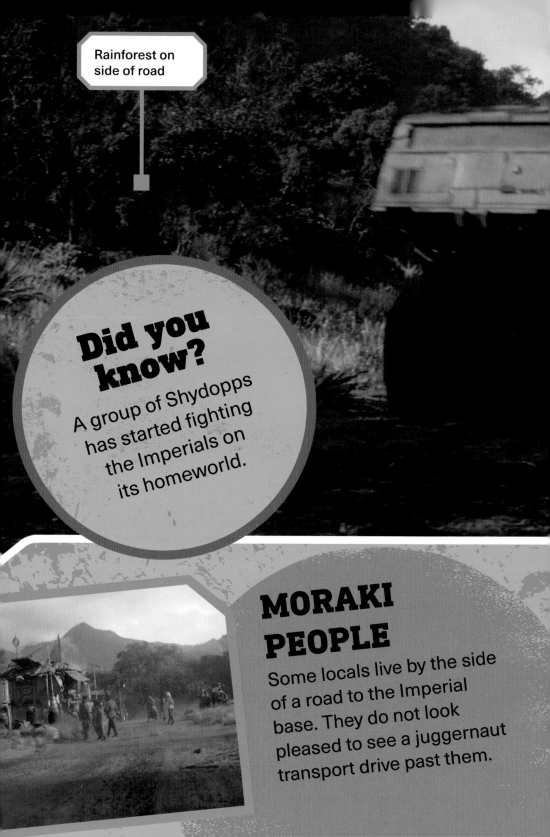

Rainforest on side of road

Did you know?

A group of Shydopps has started fighting the Imperials on its homeworld.

MORAKI PEOPLE

Some locals live by the side of a road to the Imperial base. They do not look pleased to see a juggernaut transport drive past them.

Juggernaut J-5 carrying raw rhydonium to the refinery

Well-worn dirt road to Imperial refinery

MORAK

Morak is a forested world with meager deposits of a valuable mineral named rhydonium. As the Imperial Remnant has to operate far from the New Republic's gaze and needs the mineral for fuel, it sets up a mine and a refinery to process rhydonium on this relatively unknown planet.

JUGGERNAUT TRANSPORTS

The HCVw A9.2 juggernaut transport is a wheeled vehicle manufactured by Kuat Drive Yards. The Imperial Remnant uses this type of vehicle on Morak, but it has no weapons so is easy to attack.

Cockpit

Loud-hailer

Heavy-duty wheels

RHYDONIUM

Rhydonium is very dangerous in its unrefined state and can explode if stored too close to repulsor technology. The Imperials move it on wheeled vehicles to avoid this.

A single well-placed shot destroys the base

MORAK BASE

The Imperial refinery is a vital part of the mining hub on Morak, so it is protected by a platoon of troopers and antiaircraft cannons. Inside the base there is an internal Imperial computer that Mayfeld can use to locate Moff Gideon's cruiser.

Fett's starship

Did you know?

The base is run by former ISB officers, so security is very hard to breach.

VALIN HESS

This ruthless Imperial general played a key role in attacks at the end of the war that caused lots of destruction. Mayfeld served under him and hated his orders.

LAMBDA SHUTTLE

The *Lambda*-class shuttle is a mainstay of the Imperial navy and is used to transport important passengers between locations. Imperial leaders Emperor Palpatine and Darth Vader used to have their own personal *Lambda*-class shuttles.

LOYAL COPILOT

Lambda shuttles can be piloted by a single individual, but a copilot often works alongside them. Unlike the shuttle's pilot, the copilot passionately believes in the Empire.

Wings in flight position

Did you know?

The shuttle's cockpit can eject from the vessel to form an escape pod.

Cockpit

Twin blasters

Did you know?

This type of ship has been in service since the Clone Wars.

Laser cannon

LAFETE DINER

Mando meets Bo-Katan Kryze and Koska Reeves in a diner on Lafete. They agree to help Mando so Bo-Katan can try and retrieve the Darksaber.

Cabin behind cockpit

Engine built into wing

GAUNTLET STARFIGHTER

The Gauntlet starfighter is a versatile type of craft designed by Mandalorians for their use. Also known as the *Kom'rk*-class fighter/transport, the ship can be used in dogfights as well as to transport warriors into battle.

GIDEON'S CRUISER

Moff Gideon uses an Imperial *Arquitens*-class light cruiser as his mobile base of operations. It is far smaller than an *Imperial*-class Star Destroyer, so is more useful for operating without drawing the attention of the New Republic.
This type of light cruiser saw action during the Clone Wars.

TIE fighter launch tube

Sensors

Port engine

Cargo areas

DARK TROOPER BAY

Moff Gideon's cruiser has a special room containing a squadron of dark troopers. They require time to charge up, but they are very difficult to defeat once active.

LUKE SKYWALKER

Jedi Knight

Luke Skywalker is a Jedi Knight who was a member of the Rebel Alliance and helped defeat the Empire. He feels Grogu's presence on Tython through the Force and tracks him to Moff Gideon's cruiser.

Things you need to know about Luke

1 Luke flies a T-65 X-wing that he has used since the Battle of Yavin nearly a decade ago.

2 He is very strong with the Force and easily beats Moff Gideon's dark troopers.

3 After the Battle of Endor, Luke trains his sister Leia to be a Jedi and hunts for lost Jedi artifacts.

4 Luke Skywalker will go on to train a number of other Jedi students, including his nephew Ben Solo.

R2-D2

Trusty astromech

R2-D2 has been operating for decades, loyally serving members of the Skywalker family. He has accompanied Luke on many of his Jedi missions, just as he served Luke's father, Anakin, when he was a Jedi Knight.

Things you need to know about R2-D2

1 R2-D2 has never had his memory wiped, which means he has developed quite a unique and quirky personality.

2 He is very smart and often figures out quick ways to help his allies.

3 R2 has traveled to many unusual places over the years, including a planet that is the homeworld of the Force.

4 He has fought in two galactic wars: the Clone Wars and the Galactic Civil War.

5 R2-D2 is equipped with many handy tools.

153

Weequay member of entourage

Twi'lek dancer freed by Fennec

JABBA'S PALACE

Twi'lek Bib Fortuna now sits atop a throne on the platform that was occupied by his former master, the criminal gangster Jabba the Hutt. Bib used to be Jabba's Majordomo and served by Jabba's side for years, but now he appears to be in command.

RETURN OF BOBA

Boba and Fennec arrive at the palace and easily dispatch Fortuna's Gamorrean guards. After killing Bib, Boba takes his place on the throne.

"I'LL SEE YOU AGAIN. I PROMISE."

– Mando to Grogu

GLOSSARY

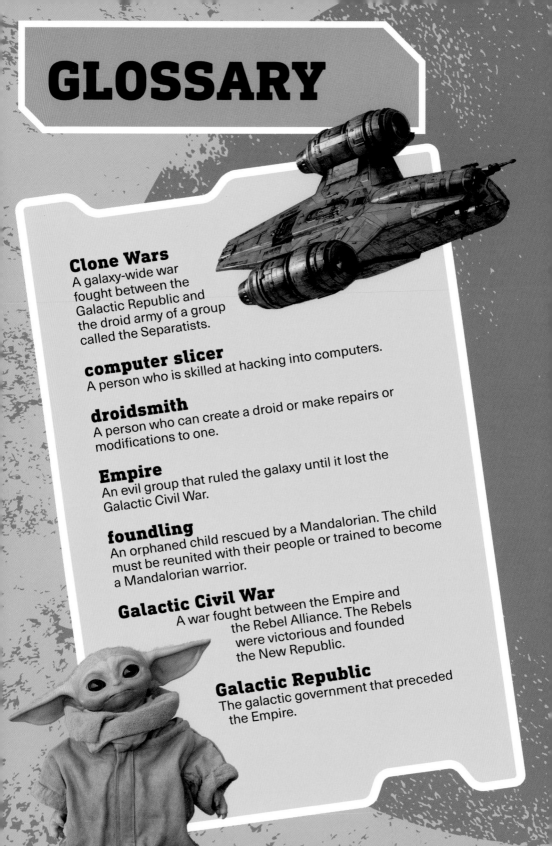

Clone Wars
A galaxy-wide war fought between the Galactic Republic and the droid army of a group called the Separatists.

computer slicer
A person who is skilled at hacking into computers.

droidsmith
A person who can create a droid or make repairs or modifications to one.

Empire
An evil group that ruled the galaxy until it lost the Galactic Civil War.

foundling
An orphaned child rescued by a Mandalorian. The child must be reunited with their people or trained to become a Mandalorian warrior.

Galactic Civil War
A war fought between the Empire and the Rebel Alliance. The Rebels were victorious and founded the New Republic.

Galactic Republic
The galactic government that preceded the Empire.

hyperdrive
A type of engine that allows a ship to enter hyperspace.

hyperspace
A special area of space that can be accessed to allow a starship to travel very quickly.

ISB
The ISB was a group within the Empire that ensured Imperial troops were loyal and found Rebel spies.

kama
A type of flexible armor worn around the legs.

Magistrate
A title for a person who leads a group of people on some planets.

majordomo
A title for a criminal boss' second-in-command.

megalith
A stone that forms part of an ancient structure.

Rebel Alliance
A group that defeated the Empire during the Galactic Civil War.

repulsor
A special type of technology that allows vehicles to hover above the ground.

DK | Penguin Random House

Edited by Matt Jones and David Fentiman
Project Art Editor Chris Gould
Senior Production Editor Jennifer Murray
Senior Producer Mary Slater
Managing Editors Emma Grange and Sarah Harland
Managing Art Editor Vicky Short
Publishing Director Mark Searle

For Lucasfilm
Senior Editor Robert Simpson
Creative Director Michael Siglain
Art Director Troy Alders
Story Group Leland Chee, Pablo Hidalgo, and Emily Shkoukani
Asset Management Chris Argyropoulos, Nicole LaCoursiere, Gabrielle Levenson, Bryce Pinkos, Erik Sanchez, and Sarah Williams

First American Edition, 2021
Published in the United States by DK Publishing
1450 Broadway, Suite 801, New York, NY 10018

Page design copyright © 2021
Dorling Kindersley Limited
DK, a Division of Penguin Random House LLC
21 22 23 24 25 10 9 8 7 6 5 4 3 2 1
001–326308–Nov/2021

A catalog record for this book is available from the Library of Congress.
ISBN 978-0-7440-4819-3

DK books are available at special discounts when purchased in bulk for sales promotions, premiums, fund-raising, or educational use. For details, contact:

DK Publishing Special Markets, 1450 Broadway, Suite 801, New York, NY 10018
SpecialSales@dk.com

Printed and bound in China

For the curious
www.dk.com
www.starwars.com

MIX
Paper from responsible sources
FSC™ C018179

This book is made from Forest Stewardship Council™ certified paper—one small step in DK's commitment to a sustainable future.